This book belongs to:

Best friends come in all shapes and sizes.
Your new best friend is waiting for you.

Mom's Big Catch

To Lucy-
Follow your
dreams! ☺
Marla McKenna

by
Marla McKenna

TATE PUBLISHING & Enterprises

Published by Tate Publishing & Enterprises, LLC
127 E. Trade Center Terrace | Mustang, Oklahoma 73064 USA
1.888.361.9473 | www.tatepublishing.com

Tate Publishing is committed to excellence in the publishing industry. The company reflects the philosophy established by the founders, based on Psalm 68:11,
"The Lord gave the word and great was the company of those who published it."

Book design copyright © 2011 by Tate Publishing, LLC. All rights reserved.
Cover and interior design by Elizabeth M. Hawkins
Illustrations by Rebecca Riffey
Author photo courtesy of Images of Waterford

Published in the United States of America

ISBN: 978-1-61777-761-5
Juvenile Fiction / Sports & Recreation / Baseball & Softball
11.04.14

To God,
for His unending favor and blessings.

To my husband, my daughters
and my parents,
for believing in me, inspiring me
and loving me always.

I jumped out of bed and ran down the stairs screaming, "It's time! It's time!" It was time to get ready for the baseball game! My big sister, Julia, and I put on our favorite baseball shirts and caps and grabbed our gloves. It was a very sunny and bright day—a perfect day. I knew my skin would burn, and my freckles would peek out if my mom didn't put sunscreen on me. It smelled like coconut, and I liked it!

I was ready to go!

"It's the last game of the season, Ashley!" my dad told me. I knew we just had to catch a ball today. I dreamed of catching a ball hit by my favorite team. I could only imagine what that would feel like. My dad said he'd been trying to catch a ball since he was a little boy. That's a long time. I hope I don't have to wait that long. It would just be so awesome to catch a ball. I would take it to school and show all my friends. I would eat with that ball! I would even sleep with that ball! My dog, Sadie, would surely try to steal that ball from me. She is my best friend and follows me everywhere. I love her a lot.

"Time to go!" shouted dad. I hugged Sadie and skipped out to the car.

It was a short ride to the stadium, but it seemed to take forever. Julia and I played slug bug to make the time go faster. "What is taking so long? Why aren't we there yet?" I impatiently asked my dad. I could almost taste that yummy and fluffy, hot buttered popcorn and feel the tingling in my mouth from that oh so wonderful, blue cotton candy. Of course we can't forget the ice cream.

I love ice cream!

Finally, we pulled into the parking lot. "Come on dad, hurry!" I shouted as we raced into the stadium. There were so many people that I held my dad's hand so I wouldn't get lost. I liked it when I walked with my dad. We rode up the escalator together, and it made me a little scared, but I was with my dad, and I was brave, so it was okay.

We got to our seats just in time to sing the national anthem. My dad, Julia and I took off our caps and put them over our hearts just like the ball players. My mom held my little sister, Emily.

Then the announcer yelled, "Play ball!" It was time to start the game! I watched the players run onto the field. They ran so fast and threw the ball so far. It was all very exciting! My favorite player got a big hit and slid into third base. Safe! I saw the umpire signal. Two runs scored, and we were already winning. I cheered! I was having so much fun, but I really wanted to catch a ball. It was all I could think about. I just couldn't get it out of my head.

As the game went on, we were getting hungry. I really wanted some popcorn or ice cream or juicy, sweet licorice. I just couldn't decide, but there was no way I was leaving the game. What if a ball was hit my way and I wasn't here? That would just be terrible.

Julia and dad went to get some snacks for us. I stayed with my mom who was still holding my little sister. Mom had some special treats for Emily that she kept in her big purse along with juice and diapers. I liked my mom's purse. It had little blue and white baseballs all over it. It didn't have a zipper or snap to close it, but that was okay. She only took this purse when we went to the ballpark, and she always kept it by her side. "Our team is up to bat," I said to my mom. "I wish Dad and Julia were back."

Just like that, a ball was hit really hard and high! "It's coming our way!" shouted mom. "It has to be a homerun!" I climbed up on my seat to get taller so I could catch it. I was ready. How would I ever catch that ball? I wish my dad was here! He would catch it for sure. Then the ball hit the bleachers and it bounced really high. Then it bounced again. Then guess where that ball landed!?

That ball landed right in my mom's big purse!

Yes! It's true! I saw it! I wished my dad was here! My mom and I looked at each other and couldn't believe it. We laughed and hugged. Then my little sister, Emily, took that beautiful ball out of my mom's purse and giggled and gave it to me.

Dad and Julia came back with popcorn and my favorite blue moon ice cream. Julia smiled and asked, "Where did you get that ball?" They were so surprised when we told them what just happened. I wished they could have seen it. I wouldn't have believed it if I hadn't seen it for myself. We were all so happy! I could see how important that ball was to my dad. I gave it to him and said, "I want you to have this ball, dad." He had waited so long for a real major league baseball. He winked at me and said, "Thanks Ashley, but it will belong to our whole family." He tapped the tip of my cap, and it went over my eyes a bit. I pushed it back up and hugged him.

I held that perfect ball all the way home. "We'll put this ball in a special place, right up on the shelf next to our family picture. But tonight Ashley, you can sleep with it!" dad said. And that's what I did.

When my dad tucked me in I said, "We are so lucky that mom brought that big, wonderful purse to the game today!"

"We sure are!" he said.

"Mom sure had a big catch!" I said as I hugged my dad. I felt very lucky and very thankful.

It was the best day of my life!

Donations:

The mission of the Linda Blair WorldHeart Foundation is to make sure that every animal they rescue is given a second chance at a happy life and a loving forever home. Thank you to all those involved in making this wonderful Foundation possible. Partial proceeds from this book are donated to their cause, with special thanks to Rick Springfield and his family for their generosity in matching this donation. Every dog deserves to be loved, and together we can all make that happen. Thank you for your support!

e|LIVE

listen|imagine|view|experience

AUDIO BOOK DOWNLOAD INCLUDED WITH THIS BOOK!

In your hands you hold a complete digital entertainment package. In addition to the paper version, you receive a free download of the audio version of this book. Simply use the code listed below when visiting our website. Once downloaded to your computer, you can listen to the book through your computer's speakers, burn it to an audio CD or save the file to your portable music device (such as Apple's popular iPod) and listen on the go!

How to get your free audio book digital download:

1. Visit www.tatepublishing.com and click on the e|LIVE logo on the home page.
2. Enter the following coupon code:
   73af-4d12-c533-f729-c93c-451d-cde1-a22d
3. Download the audio book from your e|LIVE digital locker and begin enjoying your new digital entertainment package today!